WANTED PANDA

igloobooks

PANDA!

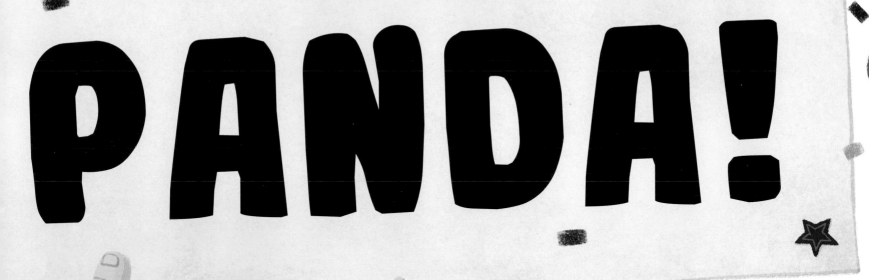

What's that?

you say.

It's a cute, cuddly friend
I can play with all day!

Erm... nice cat?
But not even close.

EEK!

No, thank you.

I want a panda.

There's no need to glare.
Okay, I'll tell you.
A panda's a BEAR.

Getting warmer!

But no, that's just
a teddy bear.

I want a panda.

You say,

Tell me more.

This kind of bear really
loves the outdoors.

Wrong again.
That's a grizzly bear.

RUN!

I want a panda.

Still you don't know?
Well, it's black and white
from its head to its toes.

Now, when did I say
anything about spots?
And that's not even a bear!

I want a panda.

I can't help!

you shout.

Okay, it likes sleeping and lounging about.

No... but can I keep hiiiim?

I want a panda.
No, don't give up yet!

A panda is

giant

and makes a great pet!

Good, we're back to bears.
But this bear's only white!

Remember what we talked about...
he likes the outdoors, cute and cuddly,
black AND white?

I want a panda.

You've got this, be strong!
This hungry bear loves
to eat all day long.

NO, silly! Now you're getting totally confused.
You've forgotten about the bear part again.

Oh, did I tell you
he eats bamboo...?